Noni Says No

Heather
Hartt-Sussman

Illustrated by
Geneviève Côté

TUNDRA BOOKS

Published in Canada by Tundra Books,
75 Sherbourne Street, Toronto, Ontario M5A 2P9

Published in the United States by Tundra Books of Northern New York,
P.O. Box 1030, Plattsburgh, New York 12901

Library of Congress Control Number: 2010926097

Library and Archives Canada Cataloguing in Publication

Hartt-Sussman, Heather
    Noni says no / Heather Hartt-Sussman ; Geneviève Côté, illustrator.

ISBN 978-1-77049-233-2

    I. Côté, Geneviève, 1964- II. Title.

PS8615.A757N66 2011   jC813'.6   C2010-902062-6

We acknowledge the financial support of the Government of Canada through the Book Publishing Industry Development Program (BPIDP) and that of the Government of Ontario through the Ontario Media Development Corporation's Ontario Book Initiative.
We further acknowledge the support of the Canada Council for the Arts and the Ontario Arts Council for our publishing program.

ONTARIO ARTS COUNCIL
CONSEIL DES ARTS DE L'ONTARIO

Medium: digital

Design: Leah Springate

Printed and bound in China

1 2 3 4 5 6   16 15 14 13 12 11

For Scotty and Jack, Ethan and Kyla.
And for Pete's sake!

– H.H.S.

For all those who had to learn how to say *no*,
yet still know when to say *yes*.

– G.C.

Noni can do lots and lots of things.

She can give her baby brother his bottle.

She can tie her own shoelaces.

She can walk to her friend Susie's house all by herself.

The only thing Noni can't seem to do is say *no*.

Noni can recite the alphabet backwards. She can count to one hundred while hopping on one leg.

She can help Mama in the kitchen and fold napkins into pretty patterns.

But Noni cannot say *no*.

When Noni was much younger, she had no trouble saying *no*.
 In fact, she almost always said *no* to her mama.

She almost always said *no* to her papa.

And she would have said *no* to her baby brother, too, if he'd been born back then!

But now, if her friend Susie asks to sleep over, Noni says *yes*, even though she sometimes wants to say *no*.

If Susie asks to play with Noni's special doll, Noni says *yes*.

If Susie asks to borrow her favorite dress, Noni says *yes*.

Noni absolutely, positively cannot say *no*.

One day, while playing hairdresser, Susie asks Noni
if she can cut her hair. She wants to take it all off,
except for a tuft at the front, and dye it red.

Noni hems and haws. She stutters and stalls. She
really, really, really wants to say *no*.

But Noni says *yes*.

Afterwards, she is very, very sorry (so is her mother)!

At Susie's house, when Noni asks if she can sleep over, Susie has no trouble saying *no*.

When Noni asks if she can play with Susie's special teddy bear, Susie says *no* without hesitation.

And when Noni asks to be the princess and wear the sparkly tiara, Susie says *no* again.

But when Susie asks to come over the very next day, Noni says *yes*, even though she wants to say *no*.

On their playdate, Susie tears a bunch of pages out of Noni's favorite book. She gives herself the leading role when they perform for Noni's brother, and, by royal decree, Noni has to play the dog.

And when Susie asks Noni if they can watch the same movie for the thousandth time, Noni says *yes*, even though she wants to say *no*.

Finally, Susie goes too far. She asks if she can stay overnight and sleep in Noni's bed while Noni sleeps on the floor.

"N...," says Noni. "N-n-n-n-n ... N-n-n-n-n-n-n ... N – OK," she says finally.

Susie sleeps very well that night.

Noni does not.

Now Noni is livid.

She is **raging MAD**.

She is **TOTALLY FUMING**.

(Not to mention very, very tired!)

When Susie asks if she can have the last bowl of Noni's absolutely, positively favorite cereal, Noni digs down deep, braces herself, inhales, and gets ready for the confrontation, the showdown, the fight to end all fights. And in her biggest, bravest voice, she finally says it:

"NO!"

"OK," says Susie. "I'll have toast."